Love Finds an Outlaw

Small Town Brides

by

Diana Lesire Brandmeyer

DKDBooks
O'fallon, Illinois

Love Finds an Outlaw

For Pastor Randy
Bolt and his wife,
Jean

Chapter One

1876 *Topeka, Kansas*

The string quartet Mary Owen's father had hired for her small birthday dinner played in the background. The receiving line thinned to a few more single men waiting for an introduction.

She'd been pleasant to each of them, asking a question to judge their excitement for adventure. None would go west, even to visit, and one thought riding the trolley thrilling. She planned on repeating the responses to her father in the morning. Proving that she had indeed attempted to find someone interesting enough to consider marrying.

"William Crossen."

Her father shook the man's hand.

"My father is a friend of Mr. Wagner."

"Yes, he told me you might be attending. Let me introduce you to my daughter, Miss Owen."

"Charmed, Mr.—"

"Wy— William Crossen, Miss Owen."

"Thank you, I've met so many for the first time tonight. Tell me, what do you think about traveling to Africa?"

"I haven't considered it. Are you planning a trip?"

His eyebrows scrunched. He didn't care for her question. She almost sighed but held back. One more handsome gentleman, but not one who would gallop beside her up a mountain or blaze trails through a forest. "Not at the moment, but asking questions helps me remember to whom I've spoken."

Attending and trying, as her father requested, to find someone she might marry was the only way he'd allow her to go with Aunt Cora on a small adventure. Even now, she had yet to see the tickets. She would get them at breakfast, if Father felt she held up her end of this event.

And she had. The gloves riding her arms up to her elbows begged to be unbuttoned, slid off, and tucked away. The dress, a breathtaking wonder Father ordered from Paris for her, held her tight at the waist. Did Queen Victoria feel like this? Bound to responsibility with cloth and silk?

Would her mother, if she had lived, understand how much Mary wanted to be like Aunt Cora? Or would Mother have trained Mary to be like her, a lady at all times, content in the life she lived?

Aunt Cora, her father's sister, bounced in and out of Mary's life with her exciting travel tales and trunks full of exotic trinkets and clothing. Her spinster life intrigued Mary.

"All you need is one, Mo." Father whispered in her ear, startling her. "Marry, and you'll be taken care of forever."

"You promised not to call me that." Mo, the nickname he used when trying to get her to follow his chosen path, his clear intention tonight. He'd combined the initials of her first and last names to get it when she fussed about not having a middle name like her friends. The problem arose when she wanted to go a different direction from his. And she did.

"I sense you are not present in your mind tonight. Why is it so difficult for you to think of being married? I'm to blame for not giving you another mother."

"Father, you say that, and yet you aren't married. Perhaps marriage isn't as wonderful as you wish me to believe."

"What you don't remember is the joy I shared with your mother. That is what I wish for you, dearest. I haven't found another who could outshine her. It wouldn't be fair to marry someone I couldn't love as much as my dear wife."

"Maybe that is my problem as well. You've made your marriage to Mother sound so perfect that I want the same. I want to love someone who loves adventure and doesn't intend for me to wed, live, and die in the same home. He isn't in this room. I wonder if he exists."

"You promised me after this trip, this adventure, you will accept someone." He gave her arm a gentle squeeze. "You will understand so much more when you have children, the need to protect them."

She met his eyes, surprised to see a bit of moisture in the corners. "I said I would try. Please, can we enjoy my birthday together? I dislike being at odds with you. Especially as you will be leaving for New York in a few days and I will be off on my grand adventure."

"You need to take care of Aunt Cora as well. That's why I'm letting you go. I'm afraid she'll skip meals and something will happen to her. Well, that's not a cheerful thought, nor is this evening turning out the way I'd hoped. We should have held this at home, with your friends."

"I see them often enough. Besides, it feels as if you've already paraded every marriageable male in St. Louis and Topeka in front of me."

"And none of them, not even one, interested you a little, Mo?" Her father led her to the dining room.

"None, Father. They were all content to stay where they were, no desire to see the world. And shallow. It's all about how they will work in the family business. If I become a missionary nun, at least I'll go places and work with God."

"You could work with a husband, help him in his career by making sure his home is run in a timely and efficient manner."

"Father, you can't be saying that as if you mean it. If you felt a wife's role crucial to a man's career, you would have remarried despite your declaration of how much you loved my mother."

"Maybe tonight will be different."

Topeka was worlds away from her life in St. Louis. In a few days, she would be on a train with Aunt Cora. Sent away again, but this time by her own choice.

WYATT RECOGNIZED THE glassy look in Miss Owen's eyes. Had she met too many people? Or perhaps, like him, she wanted to be elsewhere? At least being a male, he had more choices than to be paraded in front of wealthy men seeking a wife.

Potted plants hugged the corners along with a few women who seemed to wear a cloak of invisibility that kept most suitors from seeing them. Was it intentional? Could there be women who didn't want to marry? According to his father all women were meant to marry. But then his father was brought up in a different time. Still tonight's attendance by so many available women made him think things might not have changed. It could be a story, but not one that he would be willing to write. Articles like that did not build a career.

The question Miss Owen asked him about Africa intrigued him, as it was far from the usual conversations he'd had in receiving lines.

Maybe he'd find a story here if he stuck it out through the evening.

MARY'S HEELS FELT THE bite of the too-tight tapestry shoes. They matched the green in her dress, and she'd been so sure they would loosen as the night went on. Her mistake now had her sitting alone next to a potted tree. Her shoulders relaxed as she took in the occupants of the room, the unmarried women huddled together, chirping like birds, probably hoping one of the eligibles would single them out. Hiding by the tree worked to her advantage.

"—leaving Sunday on the Pueblo Excursion train." A male voice with a touch of excitement continued. "Should be quite the adventure."

She caught the words and held them close. Did Father have anything to do with this?

Chapter Two

As Mary approached the dining room the next morning, Aunt Cora's voice drifted down the hall. When she heard her name, she paused to listen.

"If you don't let Mary go, you'll drive her to the jungles in Africa."

"Why would you think that, Cora?"

"Have you not paid any attention to your daughter these past two years? She reads those missionary magazines over and over."

"It's a passing fancy. Saving the world is nothing more than a fantasy. Once she marries and has children of her own—"

Mary wanted to rush in and explain that it wasn't a childhood dream, but she held back.

"What if she doesn't?"

"Last night she might have met someone. I saw her chatting with a few men who would make decent husbands."

"By your standards. What if she wants to marry for love? Have you even asked her?"

"Nonsense. We've discussed her need to marry. Love hasn't come into the conversation. She doesn't have to live the way you do, Cora."

"Brother, that's incorrect and you know it. You know why I chose this life. You might as well put her on a ship to Africa tomorrow if you aren't going to let her go with me on this excursion."

"Cora—"

"No, I don't want to hear your excuses. When a telegram arrives saying she has been eaten by cannibals or lost her leg because of a snake bite, remember you could have prevented it."

Cannibals! Mary covered her mouth.

SQUARING HER SHOULDERS and preparing for battle, Mary entered the dining room. Aunt Cora sat across from Father.

"We didn't wait for you, dear. We thought you might sleep in this morning after last night's event."

"The pancakes and sausage are quite good, Mo." Her father pushed back in his chair. "I've had a few too many."

Mary filled her plate from the buffet. She had to go on this trip. If she built on what Aunt Cora said about being a missionary, it might sway her father.

At the table, her father stood and pulled out her chair. "Your aunt and I were discussing the trip."

"Yes, Father?" She sat and put her napkin in her lap. "I did what you asked. I met every male in Topeka last night."

"Did you find any that you'd care to see again?" He picked up his coffee cup and drank.

"There were so many, and they all seemed the same. Boring. Not one took me seriously when I asked about going west or liking adventure."

"That's good. It means they were stable, good providers. They won't be wandering off, leaving their family to fend for themselves." He set the cup on the saucer. The coffee sloshed, breaching the rim.

"You've taught me how to shoot, Father. I think I can take care of myself. If I don't marry, I won't have to protect a family." She sliced though the pancake and then stabbed it with her fork. He wasn't going to let her go with Aunt Cora.

"Brother, this is nothing more than a quick trip to the Colorado Territory. Let her go so she can see what adventure is about." Aunt Cora placed her hands in her lap. "Mary, you'll consider your father's request? On this trip, will you think about the men your father presented to you, what they can offer you, and give your father an answer when we return?"

Her pancake swelled in her mouth. She chewed. She could do this, take the trip and decide later. She nodded.

"That's the best I can hope for, then. Mo, you may go, but you must take care of your aunt. Truly, this is the real reason I can give for acquiescing to your request. Your aunt must eat often or, as you know, she passes out."

"Really, Brother, I am quite capable of feeding myself."

"But if something was to go wrong—"

"I promise to take care of her, Father."

His shoulders sagged. "Then I will allow this trip." He reached into his suit pocket and withdrew the train tickets. He set them on the table. "I'm not fond of this idea, but if you promise to consider marriage when you return, you have my blessing."

Mary's heels bounced against the carpet. Should she run to her father and hug him? She stilled her feet. She wasn't a little girl anymore. He needed to see that. "Thank you, Father. I will do as you ask." Then, before he could change his mind, she reached over, grabbed the tickets, and placed them in her lap.

"It's going to be a grand adventure, Aunt Cora."

WYATT CROSSEN LEANED against the edge of the pocket door of his father's office after dinner. He crossed his arms waiting for his father to criticize his choices.

When his mother excused herself for the evening and his father suggested they go into the library for a discussion, he knew his father would issue another demand concerning his life.

His father sat in the largest chair by the fireplace. "Come, sit."

With heavy feet, he made his way to the smaller chair, his mother's. Did it make her feel as unequal as it did him?

"It's time you find a wife."

And there it was, the biggest demand of all.

"I'm not ready. I can't support a family on my wages."

"You could, if you worked for me." His father tapped the armrest.

"We've been through this argument. I want to write, not work with numbers in a ledger. It's important to me to make my own way in this world." He regretted his words, knowing they would open a sore that refused to heal.

"Are you saying I didn't?" His father pounded his fingers against the wood.

"No, Father. Without you, the business would have failed, but the difference is you wanted to work in the shipping business. My heart doesn't lie there." And it never would. If only he could make his father understand. "Was there ever a time you wanted to do something else?"

"I did what was expected of me. My heart never strayed."

His father stared past him. Was he lying? "Never?"

"It's bad enough you work for that paper, but to refuse to marry is unacceptable. This family needs an heir. You are the only son. Do you understand it is your duty to provide one?" His father's cheeks flushed, cranberry red next to his white beard.

"Father—" Wyatt leaned forward, gripping the armrests.

"I'm not finished. No one in this family has worked with his hands since your great-great-grandfather bought the shipping company. You are too much like your mother's family, living life through God, letting Him direct all your actions." He punctuated his words with a wave of his hand. "Well, son, that will not get you where you need to be in this life. Just look at them. Preachers and farmers. That's all they will ever be."

Wyatt disagreed. Perhaps his father hadn't worked with his hands, but those before him had. His grandfather told him stories about sailing on the ships, what it was like to be on the ocean in a storm, and in a country where English wasn't spoken. As for letting God direct his actions, that wasn't going to change.

"I sent you to the Wagners' last week. Did you find at least one woman you could imagine being married to?"

"I went because you requested it, but again, Father, I will marry someone I love, a woman God made for me to be my helpmate." Miss Owen had surprised him with her question about Africa, but she was from a Trenton and would return there. Besides, he'd be off in a few days himself. It did seem as if God placed interesting women in his path but then swept them away before he could pursue them.

"Pure foolishness. But realize you and any children you sire will be penniless if you don't marry this year."

"That may be, but I won't dishonor God by making a mockery out of one of His sacraments. I trust He will provide what my family will need."

"What about 'Honor your father?'" Father fisted his fingers and pounded the armrest.

"That's what I did this past Saturday evening by attending the Wagners' function. Along with that, I write under the pen name Wyatt Cross, as you insisted, in addition to a host of other demands these past years." And he'd become used to that name.

"Is it so hard for you to stay in Topeka? For your mother's sake?"

"Not as long as I am free to travel." His father brought out an immature side of him. He knew why marriage and staying in Topeka were important to his parents. Knew it too well. He'd heard so many times growing up how he was a miracle. Their only child. Though his mother called him a blessing from God, his father seemed to think having William was a right in life.

"You aren't our prisoner, William. With the money we have, you could travel anywhere you choose." He slumped in his chair. "We're growing old too fast. Someday you'll understand." His father rubbed his balding head.

"I'm sorry. I know you wish the best for me and always have. I'll consider what you are asking and continue to pray for God to soon send the one He has chosen for me."

A muscle ticked in his father's jaw. "God again."

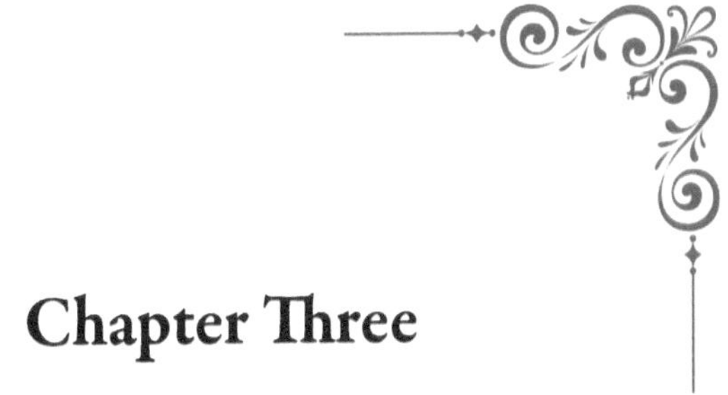

Chapter Three

Mary stood on the platform waiting to board the Pueblo Excursion train. She shivered in the March wind despite the woolen traveling suit she wore. No, it wasn't from the cold. Excitement coursed through her, sending goose bumps down her spine. She was really doing this. Her first adventure, and if she could get Aunt Cora's secret from her, it would not be the last.

"Mary, stop bouncing." Aunt Cora touched Mary's arm. "It's a train ride—"

"Not an elephant ride in India. I know. But to me, it's as exciting. Imagine being cooped up in boarding school for years, Aunt Cora. The only time I had fun was at home when Father let me practice shooting. You were so fortunate that you didn't have to endure the life I've had."

"Yes, your life has been horrible. Attending school must have been similar to incarceration." Aunt Cora scowled.

"But it was. We were told when to eat, when to sleep, and when to pray." Mary knew many girls would've been happy to go to school. But all she'd ever wanted to do was grow up at home and experience all St. Louis had to offer. Her father's ideas about appropriate experiences differed from hers. If he would have let her, she would have volunteered at the orphanage. Instead, he sent her away to boarding school. He might as well have kept her locked up.

"Protecting you," he'd said. From what, she had no idea.

She wanted to travel the world. Her father wanted her to be a wife. They'd been at odds for months. When Aunt Cora had suggested Mary come with her on the excursion to see what else life offered, Father's eyes had narrowed before he'd said no. Then Aunt Cora told him about her illness and how she needed a companion on this trip. He relented.

"It hasn't been a dull life from what you've said in your letters," Aunt Cora said.

"Schoolgirl fun and pranks, and no, I didn't come up with them. Not all of them. It doesn't compare to the excitement you've had, Aunt Cora."

"You have no idea what I have endured, Mary."

Mary chose not to reply, even though she disagreed. Today was a joyful day. Even the rumble of the baggage carts reminded her of low laughter. So many people gathered on the platform and beyond it would be impossible to count all of them. Men, of course, outnumbered the women from what she saw, but there were more than she'd expected.

The crowd came to a halt. Mary overheard a couple close to them talking. She turned slightly to see them, surprised to find them head to head whispering and smiling. They traveled together? And were happy? She couldn't pull a memory of her mother and father ever doing that.

"Get your Pueblo Excursion photo made here." A photographer stood in front of a drooping banner displaying a steam engine in front of a mountain. "Remember this trip forever!"

"Let's do it, Aunt Cora." Mary swayed and clapped her hands. Her purse swung from her wrist, almost hitting her chin. "I'm sure I'll never forget this trip, but it would be nice to have a memory to pull out and look at."

"Goodness gracious. It's a good thing I'm holding our dinner basket, or you'd have it smashed and upside down by now. You must settle down. We can get the picture taken, and by then, it should be time to board."

Mary straightened her back and forced herself not to run to the photographer. She didn't wish to embarrass Aunt Cora, especially if she hoped to travel with her again. She would act the perfect lady she'd been trained to be.

WYATT CROSS JUMPED from the buggy as it arrived at the station, overnight case in hand. He'd procured a ticket for the excursion by chance. He saw the ad and approached his editor about doing a story. He would be one of many reporters onboard, but he doubted their mission would be the same as his. There were 446 people on this train, but he wasn't interested in why the men took the trip. The women. That's where the stories would be, and, if God was listening, a wife for him.

His bag held tight in his hand, he looked for a porter. It was a two-day trip, but he needed to look good when he arrived in Pueblo, so he'd brought an extra suit. There would be cameras at the other end, and he didn't want to show up in the newspaper his father read looking unpresentable. It would only strain their relationship further.

"May I help you with that, sir?" An employee of the train company appeared in front of him. "Bound for Pueblo?"

"Sure am, George. Take care of this for me?"

"May I see your passage ticket, sir?"

Wyatt pulled the colorful ticket from his coat pocket.

George returned the ticket along with a numbered metal check. "Only one stop along the way. Your bag will be waiting at the hotel for you when you arrive."

"Thank you." Wyatt handed the man a few coins and received a wide grin in return.

"Get your picture taken before you board the train! Remember your—" A shout drew Wyatt's attention away from the attendant. He was about to dismiss the hawker when he noticed a young woman and her companion conversing with the photographer.

The young one, with hair the color of untarnished copper, smiled so hard her cheeks would hurt by the end of the session. He'd seen her before, but where? The older one, maybe her mother or aunt, showed no excitement. Bored, maybe? From her outfit, Wyatt would guess she'd been on many more exciting journeys and this one didn't compare.

So those were two of the eighty-three women on the trip. He'd start his interview with them.

MARY TOOK IN THE CLAMOR around her. They got their photo taken right away. It was good she'd urged Aunt Cora to act, or they'd be standing in the line that formed.

"Ladies, you won't regret having this beautiful reminder in the years to come." The photographer placed them close together under the banner. "Give me your basket and hand luggage. You don't want that in your photo."

Aunt Cora handed it over. "Mind you be careful of that."

"I will, madam. And miss, what about your umbrella?"

"It's part of my traveling costume."

The photographer nodded, then stepped to the edge of the photo prop and set down the basket. Once he moved behind the camera, he slipped under the dark cloth.

"Thank you for doing this, Aunt Cora."

The photographer poked his head from under the cloth. "Get a little closer to each other, please, and stand very still."

Mary brushed up closer to Aunt Cora until their shoulders touched.

"Hold still just a little longer."

Out of the corner of her eye, Mary glimpsed a flash of green as a child ducked off with their dinner. "Stop, thief!" She fled after him, ignoring the calls of the photographer and her aunt. She had to catch the robber or they wouldn't have a meal on the train. She wove through the crowd, shouting as she went. "Excuse me!"

The crowd parted, but no one stepped forward to help. There wasn't time to purchase another meal, and she had no intention of letting the boy steal it from them. Aunt Cora had to eat or she would faint. Mary promised Father she'd take care of his sister, and if that meant chasing a child, then she would.

There, a green jacket in front of her. She'd caught him. She leapt across the remaining space between them. Her motion knocked the boy to the ground. Mary wobbled but kept her balance.

"That's mine!" She leaned over him, placed her foot on his leg, and yanked the package from him. "Stealing is wrong, and stealing from women is even, even more wrong."

She nudged the boy with her umbrella. "The Bible says thou shall not steal—"

The umbrella handle slid through her hand.

Gasping, she turned her head. Another thief? A man towered over her. His mustache quivered. Was he angry? Her knees trembled. Would he strike her? Was this one of those incidents Aunt Cora told her to be aware of, where one person acted as a decoy and the other stole your money? She stood taller. "He stole—"

"He's probably hungry, miss. I'm sure he'll apologize if you let him off the ground. Won't you, son?"

Her face heated with embarrassment at the compassion and maybe something more in his voice. "I can handle this. I do not need your help."

The boy tugged her skirt. "Missus, I'm sorry. I am hungry. My sister is, too. I promised her I'd find food."

"You sit still, and be quiet." She kept her foot on the boy and stared at the man in front of her. Did she know him from somewhere? Then again, Father introduced her to so many men she couldn't be sure. It wouldn't do if word of her behavior made it back home. Gathering her thoughts, she stilled her emotions and directed her attention to the boy. "How old are you?"

"I don't have to tell you."

"Where is your sister?" The boy couldn't be more than eight. The whistle blew its boarding signal. She didn't have time to help this child right now. His clenched lips said he wouldn't give her any information.

She couldn't fix everything, but today, she could help this boy. She opened the basket and withdrew a sandwich, then an apple, and handed them to the boy. "Share this with your sister."

"Thank you. God bless." The boy stood, swayed on his feet, ready to run.

"Go on." He didn't need more encouragement. He scampered away without looking back. It concerned her that he might not have enough to feed both him and his sister. She should have given him more. Father said she shouldn't have such a soft heart for beggars, that they took advantage of her. Still, how did one know if a child was truly in need?

"That was nice of you, though he may not have a sister."

She bristled at the man's warning comment. So much like her father. "But he might. I'll take my umbrella, thank you. I have a train to catch."

Chapter Four

"Mary, I had to pay for that picture, and I'm sure it is ruined." Aunt Cora's heavy eyebrows almost knotted together as they got into the boarding line. "I would have thought better of you. Running after a basket of food as if you hadn't just had breakfast."

"I'm sorry, Aunt Cora. I had to save our dinner. You have to have something to eat." Mary handed her the basket and straightened her suit jacket. "Some of this is a bit mushed with all the jostling."

"Dear girl, this is an adventure. If it is mush, then that is what you eat. If the child had absconded with it, then that would also be part of the story you get to tell after the trip. Adventure isn't about the place you end up. It's the trip you take to get there." Aunt Cora shrugged. "Maybe you aren't ready for this."

"But I am. I was shocked someone would steal our food." Mary wanted to go back and change her actions toward the boy. She could have given him her entire portion and kept Aunt Cora's. That skinny youth in ragged clothes and bony hands might not have eaten in days, though it hadn't slowed him down. Or maybe it was the idea of eating that gave him the burst of energy to run. She did catch him.

She glanced behind her to see if she could spot him. If she remembered his face, when they returned... She stopped when her gaze collided with that odious man who took her umbrella. Was he going to Pueblo, too?

Before she turned away, he winked. Her heart kicked against her chest. Should she mention it to Aunt Cora? Or maybe she'd accept her aunt's advice and see where this journey took her. After all, he was taking the excursion trip. Perhaps he liked adventure.

She risked another look. The man held a notebook and scribbled. A reporter. Probably the excursion train would be loaded with them. She dismissed entertaining any more thoughts about him. Father would have a fit if she so much as spoke to the man again. He wouldn't be rich enough to placate her father.

WOMEN OF ALL BACKGROUNDS boarded the train in Topeka, Kansas. The first line of an article could be tricky. He'd likely change it after he spoke with some of the women. Wyatt scribbled a few more sentences about leaving the depot and the weather. He glanced up to find the copper-haired beauty who gave food to the boy staring at him. He flashed a wink and a smile. He shouldn't have, but the temptation to tease her was too great.

He'd have to find her on the train and interview her. Must be a good story there. Socialite on the Excursion. Possible heading for the article? Plucky woman to chase a child. Most of the women he knew would have screamed and pointed for someone else to do the running.

He checked the line behind him. Women were scarce in this monochromatic crowd but easy to pick out with their colorful hats. They traveled in small groups or with a husband. What would it be like to share adventures with a wife? He would concentrate on speaking to the ones without a male companion.

Wyatt closed his notebook and slipped it into his pocket along with the pencil. The line inched forward. Noticing everyone in front of him carried a package or basket onboard, he realized he hadn't stopped to pick up food for himself. His stomach growled. He woke too late for breakfast and skipped lunch. If he wanted dinner, he needed to act fast.

The line stretched behind him. Would he have enough time to purchase something at the station? He decided to risk it. "Pardon me." He moved through the murmuring crowd and ran for the depot. There wouldn't be time for the staff to make a sandwich. If he asked for a hunk of cheese and bread, and the wrapping, he would save time.

Once inside, he rushed to the lunch counter. No one stood behind it. He glanced around for an employee and then saw the sign.

Closed.

He forgot it was Sunday.

MARY WAITED UNTIL AUNT Cora's dress hem dragged the top step of the passenger car before she followed. Her shoe clunked against the steel. This was real. She relaxed as she passed through the vestibule doors.

The porter took their lunch and hand baggage from Aunt Cora and then led them down the wooden aisle. After he stored the items on the rail above the seats, Aunt Cora tipped him. "Thank you, George."

George nodded and moved a few steps back so they could sit.

"Mary, come by the window so you can see everything." Aunt Cora stepped aside as Mary slid past.

"Thank you. It will be exciting to see what the Kansas and the Colorado Territory scenery is like." Mary settled into her seat. "How did you know his name is George?"

"I don't. It's what is done on trains. Call the porter George and tip him well, and you'll always have a friend on the train. It's something I learned from my travels. I believe it has something to do with George Pullman, the owner of the trains."

"Interesting. I'll remember that." Mary peered out the window. The once-overflowing platform emptied as passengers boarded the train. There were a few stragglers. One man came running. She leaned closer to the window. The man who'd taken her umbrella. He should have been onboard by now.

The whistle sounded. Steam released. "All aboard." The conductor sounded off. "Last call."

Would he make it? Her heart jumped. It would be awful to miss this train. Especially if he was to be writing about it.

"What are you gawking at?" Aunt Cora leaned over Mary's shoulder.

Lavender essence, Aunt Cora's favorite scent, freshened the air, but it didn't calm Mary's excitement.

"I'm watching people run to catch the train. Why don't they arrive on time? Do you suppose they had an emergency? Or maybe forgot something?" Mary pressed her face against the window, trying to spot the man boarding.

She'd lost him. Just as well.

"Possibly both. Some like to test the fortitude of others' patience." Aunt Cora settled back into her seat. "I missed a train once in Spain."

Mary whipped around. Aunt Cora had the best stories. "Why?"

"Someday I'll tell you the whole tale. It isn't that exciting. We were at a café, and they had the best paella. We lost the time in laughter." Aunt Cora sighed.

"We? Who were you with?"

"Another time, dear. Another time." Aunt Cora wiped a tear from her eye.

Chapter Five

The train whistle blew. Black smoke plumed into the air. Wyatt ran, regretting the idea to go for food and thankful he'd decided to send his valise to the baggage car. Panting, he grabbed the handrail with both hands as the wheels turned. He swayed on the bottom step as the train picked up speed. That was too close.

Missing this train could have ended his career or at least demoted him from reporter to selling papers on the street. And that would have forced his father's hand. He swallowed back his anger at being ordered around.

"Ticket, sir?" The porter stood at the doorway just far enough back for Wyatt to enter the car. He spotted a purple hat and the copper tendrils of the woman he sought, sitting in the seats that faced each other. The one place he hated. There would be no leg room, but the chance to talk to these two women came before comfort.

"Got it right here, George." He slipped his ticket from his pocket and handed it over with a few coins.

"This car is pretty full. If you'd like to look in one of the others—"

"This one will be fine. I can move later if I'm uncomfortable." He took back his ticket and stuffed it in his pocket. Resisting the urge to whistle, he strode down the aisle, keeping his balance like a sailor at sea, and slid into the seat in front of the most beautiful woman he'd ever seen. How had he missed the green of her eyes when he took the umbrella from her?

Those same eyes looked loaded with ammunition and ready to take him out.

"What are you doing?" Her face reddened.

Did she think he was here to berate her about the child?

"I needed a place to sit, and this seat was open."

Her mouth formed a small *O*, but no words, not even a breath, left her lips. He seized the moment before she might ask him to move. "I'm Wyatt Cross from the *Daily Commonwealth*. I'm hoping to ask you a few questions for a column I'm writing."

"Aunt Cora?"

Good. Now he knew the relationship between them. He stared at the aunt and waited for her reply. Listening, not talking, brought him the best stories.

Aunt Cora patted her niece's hand.

A nice hand, he noticed, smooth and without a blemish, her nails trimmed to exactness.

"Mary, it's your chance to be part of history. Why don't you help this handsome gentleman with his article?"

Mary nodded. "I'm Miss Owen. It's nice to meet you."

So, she wasn't going to tell her aunt about their earlier incident. She didn't appear to remember him from the Wagners' dinner party. The woman who asked him about Africa now sat in front of him. God giving him a chance at the one he thought long gone?

"Thank you for agreeing to talk with me. Where are you from?"

"We're from St. Louis." Her voice was soft against the clacking of the wheels on the track.

"How did you get tickets for the excursion?" He leaned forward to hear her answer.

She pressed against the seat. "I'm not sure." Her eyebrows knit together, and she glanced sideways at her aunt, then back at him. "Father bought them at the depot, or did you, Aunt Cora?"

Aunt Cora coughed. "Yes, we both did in a way. I told your father I was going, and he procured the tickets."

"He must have thought you would be safe with all the dignitaries on this trip." He'd have to do some digging when he returned to Topeka. The man had connections to be able to get tickets for the excursion. But why would he send his daughter and aunt on a trip that hadn't been tested? "The excursion is the first for the Santa Fe to Pueblo; there could be problems. You must be brave women to take a journey that hasn't yet been experienced by men."

"We both like adventure, or rather my aunt does. This is my first trip. I am going to enjoy it."

"As long as things go well, I assume?" Wyatt scribbled *first-time traveler.* This would be a story to follow up on if all didn't go smooth on this first train journey to Pueblo.

"Even if they don't, Mr. Cross."

MARY HELD TIGHTLY TO the edge of the seat. Mr. Cross made her squirm. The space between their legs had to be less than two fingers' width. Her skirt moved as he adjusted his feet.

"It's a bit cramped in these seats. I apologize for mussing your outfit."

Her face warmed, and it wasn't from the woodstove in the corner across from them. She scooted her feet under the seat and smoothed the fabric a bit tauter. "Maybe you could find another place to sit?"

He twisted his body and peered down the aisle, his foot stretched to the side. Once again, he touched her hem.

"Looks pretty full to me. They sold all the tickets, and with only ten coaches there aren't a lot of open seats. I think I'll be here until we stop in a few hours." He sat back in his seat and scribbled in his notebook.

What was he writing now? She leaned forward a tiny bit, pretending to adjust her skirt while hoping for a glance at the paper. Or was he sketching?

He looked up.

She snapped back into place. His Wedgewood-blue eyes and coal-black lashes connected to some feeling she hadn't felt before, not at all unpleasant. Her breathing quickened. Perhaps if she thought of him as a restless child instead of a handsome gentleman, it would be easier to sit across from him until the next stop. He looked as disheveled as a boy.

His coat, while of good quality, had sleeves a bit too long, adding to the childlike vision. One of his light brown waves slipped through his pomade and twirled to the side. She bit back a smile. It wouldn't do for him to think she found him amusing.

"Mary, look." Aunt Cora nudged her shoulder with hers. "Is that snow falling?"

The sky grew dark, and white flakes stuck to the window.

"SNOW ISN'T UNUSUAL for Topeka in early March." Weather. He was a reporter and that's the most interesting thing he could say? Wyatt struggled for something more thought worthy to jump the conversation to his desired topic.

"We have snow in March as well, Mr. Cross. Sometimes so much the roads are impassable. Isn't that right, Mary?" Aunt Cora rubbed her forehead. "I do believe I'm getting a headache."

And he'd lost the train right off the track. Now the women were going to discuss aliments. Perhaps he should search for another seat with a woman capable of conversing about more than aches, pains, and hunger.

"Aunt Cora, it's too early for dinner, but maybe all this excitement has left you a bit hungry. Should I get you something from the basket?"

"I'll be fine, dear. Let's just give it some time and see if it disappears. Now, Mr. Cross, how did you get started in the newspaper business?"

Taken aback by her question, Wyatt almost told her he'd begun his profession as a way to irritate his father. "I've always liked to write stories, and this was a way to make my own money."

"So you come from a moneyed family, then?"

Mary's attention turned from her aunt to him. Wyatt's throat closed. Another woman looking for a husband. He'd been mistaken to think she came on this trip for the adventure.

"What makes you think that, Mrs.—" He realized she hadn't introduced herself.

"Miss Owen as well. I've never married." She turned away. "Maybe we should ask George to get the basket."

The younger Miss Owen glared at him. He'd made her angry by upsetting her aunt.

"I can retrieve it for you, Miss Owen." He stood, smashing the younger Miss Owen's dress again. If he kept this up, he'd have to buy her a new one.

"Mr. Cross, if you trample my skirt any more, you're likely to put your boot through it. We can call George to help, and maybe you can find another place to sit." She gave him a candy-sweet smile. "Then my poor unmarried aunt can rest. Your attempt at polite banter has most likely caused her a powerful headache." With that, she punched the buzzer by the window for George.

Eager to be away from the bothersome Miss Owen, Wyatt nodded. Once more, words escaped him.

He ambled down the aisle and paused next to an empty seat beside a young woman who sat next to an older man. Maybe she would be willing to talk. "May I sit here?"

The woman batted her eyes at him. His heart sunk. A woman looking for a husband.

"Of course. I'm Winnie Periwinkle, and this is my uncle Albert."

"Mr. Cross. I'm doing an article for the paper about women on the excursion. Would you mind answering a few questions?"

Miss Periwinkle brushed her shoe along his ankle then rested her foot on top of his. "What would you like to know?"

Trapped. Was this how Miss Owen had felt?

Chapter Six

Wyatt lurched across the platform to the next car. The rushing wind slid under the awning and attempted to steal his hat. He grabbed it before it took flight, holding it tightly to his head as he entered the car. The warmth from the stove hit him, and he relaxed.

He had no intention of finding a wife on this trip, despite his moment of insanity when he noticed the stunning Miss Owen's eyes. No, thank you. He'd take his father's anger. He didn't need the family money or the name. He definitely didn't need Miss Periwinkle either, despite her willingness to answer any question he asked. Her desperate friendliness had him asking a few rapid-fire questions so he could escape her obvious desire for a husband.

He strolled through the swaying car. Happy excursioners filled all the seats. He might as well return to the one he'd left. He resolved to ignore the green-eyed beauty and watch the scenery go by.

He turned to go back. The train had slowed. That wasn't right. He glanced out a window. Snow still fell, but that shouldn't affect the train. What was happening? The reporter's blood raced through his veins. He smelled a story brewing.

He took off toward the engine where he could get answers. Thoughts of his father, marriage, and money dissipated with each step he took.

"AUNT CORA, WHAT A DREADFUL man." Why had they sat so near the stove? Mary traced her cheek close to her hairline, making sure no perspiration made an appearance.

"You'll have to get used to those who are a bit rough around the edges if you want to see the world. If you're serious about missionary work, you'll stand in front of bulls who don't wish you to be in their community."

Mary handed her aunt a cookie. "Will one be enough, do you think?"

"I suppose we'll find out. It is an odd thing that eating keeps me on my feet, or in this case, on the seat." Aunt Cora sniffed the cookie. "I do love the smell of butter and sugar. Many times while in Europe, I longed for a bit of an American cookie."

"Their treats are quite delightful, but I understand. Do you feel it is because it's a memory of home more than the cookie itself?"

"Perhaps."

Mary kicked her hem out in front of her a bit to inspect the damage left by Mr. Cross's boot. A parade of dusty sole marks marched across the bottom. She would have to brush the skirt when they stopped for the night. The realization crushed her hope of an evening of leisure. "Do you encounter many like him on your travels?"

"A few, and sometimes the ones I thought were the worst of scoundrels turned out to be the nicest of gentlemen."

"Tell me about one of them, please?" She patted her aunt's arm. She loved her stories. While at boarding school, she'd retold her roommates the stories over and over. They all dreamed of living like her aunt, though they knew they would not. All of them were destined to marry a man who would improve their families' positions or coffers.

All except her. She intended to live a rich and exciting life, the way her aunt did. She refused to be sent away to a loveless marriage to lose herself because her father deemed a union more important than who she was.

"There was a young man in Spain. Why is the train slowing?" Aunt Cora wrinkled her forehead.

"We aren't to our stop yet." Mary tried to peer around her aunt to judge the reaction of the others.

The murmur from the passengers built. A woman clung to Mr. Cross. She held on to him as if she'd known him for a long time. Mary fisted her hands tightly enough for her fingernails to bite her palms.

MARY SUCKED IN A BREATH as Wyatt slid back onto the bench across from her. "It appears there is a problem up ahead."

"Why aren't you sitting with your friend?"

"Miss Periwinkle? We are acquainted but not friends. I prefer to be here where I can have the entire seat to myself. As I was saying—"

"What's happening?" Mary couldn't keep her hands still, plucking at her skirt and then her hair. "Are we in danger?

There aren't train robbers, are there?" She peered through the window and saw little but snow.

"Seems the snow has caused a problem farther up the line." Wyatt spoke loudly and intentionally.

"How do you know?"

He put his finger to his mouth as if to shush her, then stood to address the car. "I've talked to the engineer. We have to stop at the next town because something happened to the snow plow."

"Do they have a place for us to stay?" Aunt Cora leaned over to Mary. "And so your adventure begins. We shall see how you stand up to changes in plans."

"I'll be fine. It's quite exciting to have things go off the rails. I mean having to stop, not the train itself. I wouldn't care for that." Mary peeked under her eyelashes at Mr. Cross. He stood there, acting important, talking to the gentleman next to them. His voice bounced around the car like a child's ball. "I know this stop. There isn't a place for everyone to stay."

He turned from her and lowered his voice. She couldn't pick up the words. But she knew enough to know she and Aunt Cora needed a plan for the night. Maybe they could sleep in their seats. Not comfortable at all, but what other choice would there be? She intended to find out as soon as Mr. High-and-Mighty sat down.

Chapter Seven

Wicker baskets crackled as their owners opened them. Was that fried chicken he smelled? Wyatt's mouth watered. Missing breakfast and lunch turned out to be a big problem.

"Stuck? The snow plow is buried?" Mary unwrapped a sandwich and handed it to her aunt.

"Eat half. I have plenty." Aunt Cora shoved the sandwich into Miss Owen's hand. "We'll be at the next town by morning, and we can get breakfast."

He could taste the saltiness of the ham piled high between bread. Would the young Miss Owen share with him the way she had the boy? He slid his pencil out from behind his ear and chewed the top while considering how much to tell the women. "We aren't going to make it that far. The engineer said two plows are ditched and one of them is halfway on the track. We're stopping in Larned until they build a temporary track."

"Mr. Cross, where is your dinner?" The older Miss Owen sounded much like his mother. "I hope the railroad has secured rooms for us there."

"I'm not hungry." His stomach roared like thunder.

"But he must be, Aunt Cora. Did you hear—"

"Mary, don't be impolite."

She tore her sandwich in half, leaving herself a mere quarter. "Here. We know you didn't bring a dinner basket with you. What were you thinking? We were told to bring a meal."

He didn't want to take it from her, but last night's dinner was a distant memory. "Yes, I knew. I forgot. I had a late night and slept too long. I missed breakfast and didn't have time to get lunch, either."

She pushed it at him. "Go on, you must eat something."

He reached for the sandwich, brushing her gloveless fingers as he did. A spark of electricity shot between them. He pulled back. Had she felt it, too? "You're cold. Why don't you change places with me, so you can be closer to the stove?" Why did he feel a need to put her comfort before his? Would he have done the same for Miss Periwinkle? He might have, not because he wanted to, but to be polite.

"I'm fine. Thank you." She took a birdlike bite.

"Reconsider, please. It will be cold by the window, and we'll all be sleeping on the train tonight." She was stubborn. He liked that.

"Aunt Cora?"

"Part of the adventure, Mary."

HE WAS RIGHT. THEY were stuck sitting on the track for the night. She chose to stay by Aunt Cora. At least they could use each other's shoulders for pillows. Mary leaned against her aunt and tried to doze.

What if they were stuck more than one day? That wouldn't happen, would it? If it did, what would they do for food? Would the railroad send another train? Maybe Mr. Cross knew.

How did he find out information before the others? Possibly because he was a reporter? What it must be like to be free to chase a story across the country? What would it be like to be married to a man like Wyatt? Would he allow her to travel with him if she married him?

Her legs tingled and numbed. She moved them but couldn't get it to stop. Much like her father's request. She'd have to answer to her father's wishes soon, but how could she marry someone she didn't know? It wasn't fair that men could choose not to take a wife. Why couldn't her father be like her aunt?

Please, God, help me find the words to explain to him how much I need, want to be different? That I want to be a part of something bigger. Helping orphan children discover who You are would work for me, if it works for You, that is. Always Your will, Father, even if it means I marry someone my earthly father has picked out for me.

Sleep would bring the morning faster, but it continued to evade her. The soft glow from the lamps along the sides of the coach didn't help. She liked a dark room when she slept.

George explained it would be best to keep them lit to protect the ladies. Mary shivered. Safety hadn't been a concern until he said those words.

Mr. Cross closed his eyes and dropped off into sleep. How did he do that? Maybe reporters were given that gift so they could be ready to follow a story at a moment's notice.

Please, God, let the train move tomorrow. She wiggled against the seat. Funny, she didn't notice how hard it was until now.

"Are you awake?" A throaty whisper came from Mr. Cross.

Mary jumped. "I thought you were out for the night."

"Seats are too uncomfortable." He straightened up and rubbed his whiskered chin. "Can I interview you? That would pass the time."

She glanced at the passengers around her. Some played cards and others bowed their heads in slumber. There would be many sore necks in the morning. "We'll disturb Aunt Cora."

"Not if we whisper."

Mary tilted her head to one side and then the other way to ease the kinks that had settled. "What could I possibly have to say that is exciting enough for you to print?"

Wyatt reached into his coat pocket and brought out his pen and paper. "Let's find out. Why are you taking this trip?"

How much should she tell him? Knowing her father might read her words gave her pause. Caution would be best. "My aunt travels all over the world. I admire her and would like to be able to do what she does. Or become a missionary. I've not been away from home before, so my father let me come this time because Aunt Cora can't be alone."

"Why not?" His knees brushed hers.

A finger of fire raced through her. Mary swallowed and pushed back into the seat.

He readjusted his position sideways. "My apologies. There isn't much room for legs."

"She forgets to eat and becomes dizzy. I'm here to make sure she has meals on time."

"Is that why you chased the boy?" He scribbled in his notebook.

"Yes. My father asked me to watch over her, and I intend to, even if that means chasing urchins." He had nice hair, though mussed from his attempt to sleep.

His pencil stopped scratching as he looked up. "So, you didn't want to take this trip?"

"I didn't know about this excursion until Aunt Cora told me a few days ago, before we left St. Louis. I'm thankful to be allowed to accompany her." Otherwise, she might be planning her wedding.

"Is it odd you were unaware of this trip? It's difficult to obtain tickets for special excursions as they sell out fast. The paper I work for purchased mine a month ago. They were sold out a week later."

"Are you suggesting my father planned for me to come with Aunt Cora before they argued about it over breakfast?" Anger erased the fire Mr. Cross ignited within her. Why would they conspire against her? She would have said yes without the subterfuge. Did Aunt Cora even need her?

WYATT'S INSTINCTIVE reporter warning bells rang in his head. He'd rattled Miss Owen. Her eyebrows twitched, and her lips turned down. Something was up, but with her lips so tight, he didn't think he'd get much from her right now.

Miss Periwinkle strolled past, leaving a scented trail thick enough to be called a rose garden.

"Excuse me, Miss Owen. Why don't you get some rest? I'll chat with Miss Periwinkle. I have a few more questions I'd like to ask her." Even though it was the last thing he wanted to do.

Her mouth opened and closed. He'd played his cards right and rendered her speechless. Good. When he returned, he might find her willing to speak to him.

Chapter Eight

Mary woke to the bright sun poking at her eyes through the window. The snow on the ground stretched for miles. She yawned and raised her arms, then dropped them down once she remembered where she was.

Aunt Cora still slept. Mary debated waking her and calling for George to get their basket down. They had a few pieces of cake left they could eat for breakfast. After that, Mary was unsure where she would find food. Maybe she shouldn't wait to try. If she did, there may not be anything. She stood and stepped over Aunt Cora's feet. Most of the passengers still dozed. The perfect time to see what was outside the door of the train and search for food.

With George's help, she tugged on her coat. "Could you direct me to the nearest place that might have food?"

"The snow is awful deep, miss. Let the men go searching when they wake."

"I fear there won't be enough. I have to make sure my aunt has provisions."

George steadied her as she stepped on the slick metal steps to disembark from the train car. The cold from the handrail seeped through her gloves. The wind blew hard, picking up the fresh snow and sending it swirling around her. A house stood about four cars away along with a windmill, and a water tower to fill the tank of the train, but she didn't see anything else. Could this be where the stationmaster lived?

She took a step, and snow circled her ankles and slid up her shins. She withheld a shriek. The cold didn't matter. Her goal was to reach that house and see if there was food to be had. Aunt Cora could not go without. Her father had been adamant.

Someone stepped out of the house onto the porch. It looked like Mr. Cross.

Had the scoundrel found a bed to sleep in? He waved at her.

"Wait! I'll bring you what I have."

Mary stopped. It would be a blessing from God if Mr. Cross had what they needed. She heard her father's voice: "…a husband can protect you." Maybe a little watching over from a man wouldn't be so awful.

As Mr. Cross approached, his footsteps crunched in the snow. He handed her a basket. "Keep this by you. It isn't a lot, so you'll have to ration between the two of you. The stationmaster offered what provisions he has. There won't be enough to feed everyone. I know your aunt needs food, so she'll be the first to get breakfast."

"We have cake. You didn't have to bring it for us." Why did she say that? "Sorry. I'm a little grumpy in the morning, especially if I haven't slept well. Thank you for thinking of my aunt."

"Women shouldn't travel without a man. They need someone to look out after them. Since your father isn't here, I've chosen to do that for you."

He might as well have slapped her face. "If it wasn't for my aunt, I would throw this at you. I can take care of myself. That's the whole point of this trip. I'm proving to my father that I don't need anyone besides God and myself to get through this life. I am capable of finding my own food."

She tried to turn, but the snow snared her foot. She fell face forward into a freezing bank. The basket flew out of her hand. Bread and apples skittered across the snow. She lifted her head to see. The precious food lay on the tracks. If she wanted to get it, she would have to crawl underneath the train, and if she did, the bread wouldn't be edible. She bit back the tears that stung her eyes.

She pushed into a sitting position. Her wool skirts, heavy with snow, made it impossible to stand. She didn't want to ask, but she had to unless she wanted to crawl to the train and have George help her. "Mr. Cross, would you please give me assistance?"

"Here. Take my hand."

She did.

He pulled her up, balancing her against his chest.

Warmth radiated from him. For a moment, she wanted to sink against Wyatt and let him take care of her and Aunt Cora.

"What are you going to do now? You're capable, so you say. What are you going to do for dinner tonight? The engineer said we won't leave until tomorrow morning. After your cake is gone, you're still going to need three more meals."

"All I need is a shotgun, and I'll get some food. I'll get a hunting party together. Tell my aunt I'll be back later." She stomped through the snow toward the stationmaster's house. She knew how to shoot, and she was going to get a gun. There would be dinner, lunch, and breakfast, too. They might get sick of rabbit, but they would have something to eat.

WYATT BIT BACK A CHUCKLE. Maybe he was right about this woman. She wasn't one to sit back and wait for things to happen or to be given to her. He would pay more attention and dig a little further into what she was like under normal circumstances, and what her desires were for the future. Meanwhile, he let her go on to the stationmaster's home.

While she did that, he'd gather a few men and join her hunting party. She had a good idea. Getting fresh meat for the day would not be a bad plan. Perhaps with the few provisions left, one of the women passengers could make some stew and stretch it further. Good gravy, now he sounded like a woman. What was happening?

One thing he knew for certain, he would avoid Miss Periwinkle the rest of the trip. She had one thing in mind. Marriage. Marriage to anyone.

He could see why she was single. She hadn't stopped talking about herself for one minute last night. She was a great candidate for an interview if one could believe a tenth of what she said. One moment she talked about wanting to climb mountains, and the next she prattled about how she couldn't wait to sit by an evening fire with her knitting. The two things were so far apart from each other, he didn't know what to make of it.

Before he boarded the train, he waited for Miss Owen to make it to the house. He wouldn't mind having to rescue her from the snow one more time. The door closed. Whether or not she would get a gun was another question. He was surprised she didn't have one on her.

"Can I help you with that, sir?" George hung on to the rail. "It's a bit slippery."

"Here's a basket of food I got from the stationmaster. It isn't much. I'm hoping you can distribute it evenly."

Wyatt handed the basket up to George, who took it and set it down.

"He has a little left, but not much. I fear once the others realize there is nothing on the train to eat, they will hit his door as well, asking for food. I'm gathering a few men from the other car to help hunt."

He grabbed the handrail and climbed the stairs. His foot slipped, but he caught his balance before he fell.

"Careful, sir. Is there something I can do to help?"

"Would you please inform Miss Owen that her niece plans to go hunting with us?"

Imagine that. A society princess out hunting in the snow. Yes, she intrigued him. He wanted to find out more.

THE WIND HAD CALMED, making it a good time to hunt. Not far from the train, Mary stood outside the circle of men. They made more noise than hens clucking for their dinner. She took a few steps away.

"Where are you going, Miss Owen?" Wyatt caught up to her. "We agreed to stick together."

"You and your posse did. I can do far better on my own."

"It's not that we can't. It's a safety issue. As long as we are—"

Mary spotted movement on the snow. She placed the repeating Winchester on her shoulder, took aim, and fired. "Got it. You were saying? I need to pick up my rabbit, if you don't mind."

"And if you go out there and someone else shoots—"

She aimed and fired again. "Sure is a lot of talking and not much hunting going on. If you and the others are going to provide food, you best be getting to it." She walked away. Miss Periwinkle could have him. Reporters, at least this one, didn't seem to be good at providing during a crisis.

"I'm coming with you. Two of us will look bigger out there and, if God is watching out for us, we won't get shot. Or you could return to the train, and I'll get these picked up and cleaned."

"And then what? You expect me to then cook them?" Which is what she intended to do, but she wanted to know what he thought.

He rubbed his whiskered chin. "Why wouldn't you?"

"Because I bagged them. That's the rule of hunting." He probably didn't think women should have the right to vote either.

"How do you know?"

"My father taught me to hunt when I was small. I would have had more to pick up if I'd had my own gun. This one is a bit too large." She rested the long barrel over her shoulder and stepped away from him. "Are you coming?"

Chapter Nine

In the car, Mary found her aunt conversing with Miss Periwinkle, who held a piece of cake in her lap.

"I've asked Miss Periwinkle to sit with us for the remainder of the trip." Aunt Cora slid over so Mary could sit.

"I hope you don't mind, Miss Owen. Your sweet aunt is such a delight. She even shared her cake with me as I had nothing left from last night." She tittered.

"That was to be for my aunt to eat. I suppose she didn't mention if she is without food she faints?"

"Mary, there is no need—"

"Why no, she didn't mention it." Miss Periwinkle's face drooped a bit, and she looked at the cake in her lap uncertainly.

"She wouldn't. But I will, so enjoy that bit of chocolate cake. Aunt Cora, you may have mine." Mary rubbed her hands together. Her feet felt like blocks of ice from tramping through the snow, but she couldn't very well remove her boots and rub them.

"We'll see. I'm not hungry at the moment. Miss Periwinkle was telling me she hoped to find a match in Pueblo."

"Or this excursion. There are some mighty fine men to pick from, like Mr. Cross. He was sitting with you earlier. What did you think of him?" Miss Periwinkle took a bite of the cake.

"I'm sure he'll return soon. He said he couldn't find another place in the other car."

Miss Periwinkle's face took on a dreamy look. "If Mr. Cross would like to sit here, there is plenty of room beside me. Mama used to say I'm light as a feather and tiny as a hummingbird."

Mary wished she would have stayed out in the cold and dressed those rabbits. Why had she let Wyatt convince her to come inside? Especially since she was mad at him for suggesting it in the first place. It would serve him right if he had to sit by Miss Periwinkle. "I'm sure Mr. Cross would be delighted to sit next to you, Miss Periwinkle. He said you were old friends."

Miss Periwinkle blushed. "He did? Wyatt is the sweetest man. I can't believe someone hasn't snatched him up for a husband since he—"

Wyatt slid into the bench seat. "Miss Periwinkle, you aren't spreading tales, are you?"

Mary noticed he kept inches between them by hugging the edge of the seat.

"Are you warm enough, Miss Owen? I can switch places with you so you'll be closer to the stove. After that spill in the snow and hunting, it wouldn't do to catch a cold."

"Mary. You were hunting?" Aunt Cora drew herself up in an opposing posture. "I promised your father—"

"So Miss Owen is a bit of an outlaw then?" Wyatt wore a huge grin as he reached for his notebook and pencil.

"I am not, sir." *Outlaw indeed.* "I had to find provisions for my aunt. Anyone would have done the same for a family member."

"I wouldn't dream of shooting an animal, Mr. Cross." Miss Periwinkle touched his arm. "Make sure you put that in your article. It's not right for women to behave so wild-like when there are men present to take care of them."

He inched farther away, half-hanging off his seat. "I disagree, Miss Periwinkle. It's good for women to know how to take care of themselves. They can be proper helpmates to their husbands and free them from worry when they must leave them alone."

"Hmpf." Miss Periwinkle crossed her arms and huddled closer to the window.

Wyatt didn't care for Miss Periwinkle. Mary warmed inside despite the outer chill on her skin. "Mr. Cross, I would love to move closer to the heat. Thank you."

OUTLAW. THAT'S WHAT he'd call her in his article. Outlaw on the Pueblo Excursion made a grand headline. Might even be front page worthy. Mary caught his attention and held it. Women like Miss Periwinkle couldn't begin to garner his attention in her presence.

Here was a woman not afraid to go into a snow-filled pasture and hunt food for her family. Did she have a sense of adventure, too, or just one of survival? One could argue both were needed, or maybe they were interchangeable.

He watched her while she chatted with Miss Periwinkle and her aunt. He shut his eyes, hoping they would think he rested. He'd rely on his memory if they said anything that he could use in his column.

"It's rather dull waiting. Isn't it?" Miss Periwinkle tapped her foot. "If we had a game to play, it would pass the time. Did you bring cards, Miss Owen?"

"She certainly did not." Mary's aunt roused from a rest she'd been taking. "We do not play games of chance in this family. I'm surprised you do, Miss Periwinkle."

"My father allows it. Parlor games are all the rage back home in Boston. There's not much else to do in the winters."

"There is always the Bible to read or stitching that can be done. My niece has been trained in the proper ways of a lady. Didn't you go away to school?"

"My parents sent me to Europe. The rules there are much different. Always an event to attend and a gentleman to take you. Why, we even snuck out of school some evenings to walk along the riverbanks. Nothing like this backward country. That's why I came on this trip. Father is traveling in the train that left behind us. He's a legislator, and he wants to open the West to more people."

She lied, and Wyatt knew it. Earlier she'd mentioned growing up in New York and traveling with her uncle. They were buying a home in Pueblo.

"What does your father do, Miss Owen?"

Mary frowned.

Would she answer? Miss Periwinkle might as well have asked Mary how much her father was worth. Wyatt's fingers itched to get at his pencil, but he remained still.

"I'M GOING TO EXPLORE the train. Would you like to come along, Aunt Cora?" Mary wanted out of the tight space and away from Miss Periwinkle's questions.

"Walking around isn't good for me." Miss Periwinkle gazed at Mr. Cross. "I tire easily."

More like she didn't want to leave Wyatt's presence. Should she stay? "Aunt Cora?"

"Go along, dear." Her aunt elbowed Wyatt. "Would you be a dear and escort my niece? She's restless. I'll stay with Miss Periwinkle. We wouldn't want her to tire herself too much."

Mary bit back a grin. Her aunt didn't want Wyatt around that woman either. But that meant her aunt did want Wyatt around her. Did she want to see her married as much as her father did? She'd dig into that subject when she came back from her walk. By then, she trusted Aunt Cora would have encouraged Miss Periwinkle to return to her own seat.

Wyatt stood. "It would be my pleasure to escort you, Miss Owen. We can walk to the observation car. Maybe we will see a patch of green or even a buffalo."

"I'd like that. I haven't seen one yet. I hoped to see all sorts of wildlife on this trip." She waited for him to get free. Miss Periwinkle moved her feet into Wyatt's path, as if she could stop him from getting away from her.

"It's a narrow walk all the way there, but I'll be right behind you. It's three cars down." Wyatt rested his hand on her shoulder.

Mary didn't mind the warmth of his hand or the fire that rushed through her. Was Miss Periwinkle green with envy?

Chapter Ten

Mary paced the empty observation car. With all the windows, it should have been pleasant and full of excursionists. Instead, the snow and the sun hiding behind clouds made for a dreary view. "How much longer do you think we will be stranded?" She stood next to the glass, but her breath fogged it, concealing her view.

"The engineer told some of the reporters the new track should be finished by tomorrow. We might be able to pull out in the morning."

Mary turned to Wyatt. "Another day?" Her voice rose in a pitch that hurt her own ears. "You knew this. And yet you closed your eyes. And went to sleep? We don't have enough food for another day."

"Let's not panic everyone. Remember, God said you can't add a day to your life by worrying." Wyatt moved closer to her.

"That's your answer? Don't cause trouble? Don't worry? It's going to be pandemonium once it's discovered. We have to do something. I'm going to gather some men to help find more game. I'm sure I can borrow the rifle from the stationmaster again."

Wyatt grabbed her by the shoulders and pulled her close. "We aren't going to starve, and you aren't going hunting again."

She pushed against his chest. But he didn't let go. "You have no right to tell me what I can do. You aren't my father or my husband. I won't sit here waiting for provisions to be brought. I have my own gun. If I have to, I'll use it."

"You brought a rifle?"

"No, this." She pulled her small pistol from her pocket. "And if you don't let go of me, I'll use it on you."

"Miss Owen. I've been looking for you." George bent over and gasped for air.

Wyatt released her, and she hid her gun in the folds of her skirt. Her heart fluttered. "What's wrong, George?"

"Your aunt fell, and we can't wake her up."

MARY RUSHED THROUGH the cars. A man played a violin, and the bow reached into the aisle, poking her in the side as she passed. "Sorry, please excuse." She took no time to look back. *Please, God, I have to get to Aunt Cora. Please let her be awake.* Had she broken the man's bow? No matter. She would find out later and make amends.

She made it to their car and stopped. Men stood in their seats. Miss Periwinkle hovered over Aunt Cora, who lay in the aisle still as death.

Wyatt bumped into her.

She bobbled on her feet.

He steadied her.

Grateful, she took strength from his strong hands on her waist. *Please, God, let her wake up. This isn't the kind of adventure I wanted, Father.* Pulling away from Wyatt's strength, she clung to God's. She knelt at her aunt's side and stroked her cheek. "How long has she been like this?"

Miss Periwinkle, white-faced and breathing shallow, gripped the seat next to her. "Miss Owen, she decided to come with you and Mr. Cross. When she stood, she dropped like a rock. Her head cracked against the edge of the bench."

"Does anyone have any honey or preserves, even sugar?" Mary, frantic for an answer, surveyed the passengers. Blank faces returned her stares. "She needs something to eat."

"We all do." Miss Periwinkle sighed. "If I'd known she was this hungry, I wouldn't have eaten the other piece of cake she offered."

Mary stiffened with fury. She wanted to yank Miss Periwinkle's ankles so she'd fall and hit her own head.

"Think, do you have a sugar cube you slipped in your pocket, a piece of candy?" Wyatt's voice boomed above her. "You there, sir. You had butterscotch this morning. There is no time to lose here."

The man came to life. "Yes, I have a piece."

"I have a bit of preserves."

Passengers sent items to Mary. She'd never had to do this before, but Father explained what needed to be done. The preserves would work fast, but she needed water or tea. "Wyatt, I need to make this thinner."

"George, bring some water, please."

Mary patted her aunt's cheek. "Please, wake up."

Wyatt took the glass from George and handed it to Mary. She spooned it into the preserves and stirred. "Lift her head please, Wyatt."

He knelt and did as she asked.

With great care, Mary dribbled bits of the thinned mixture into her aunt's mouth. "Come on, Aunt Cora. Open your eyes."

MARY'S AUNT MOVED, and Wyatt breathed a sigh of relief.

"What's the meaning of this? Why are you all looking at me?" She coughed and then groaned. "My head."

"Be still, Aunt Cora. I'll help you back into your seat. You fainted, and now you have a nasty bump on your head."

Wyatt slid his arms under Miss Owen's. "Sorry, ma'am, but this is the easiest way since you're stuck between the seats."

"No harm, Mr. Cross. It's nice to have such a strong young man to help Mary through this." She staggered on her feet. "I think I'm fine now."

"You are not fine. I need to find you something else to eat before you have another accident. Mr. Cross, do you suppose you can rally the men for another hunting party?"

"Mary, you are not going out there again. I will not have my niece acting like an outlaw. Those men can hunt just as well as you. Besides, I'd like to have you by my side as I feel a bit weak, and Miss Periwinkle isn't much use."

"I'm sorry. If you'd have said you need the cake—"

"You shouldn't have asked." Mary thundered. "What were you thinking? That you are the only person who is hungry?"

Wyatt backed away. This outlaw was a bit more than he could handle. She didn't need a husband. She was ready for adventure. Maybe a little too much.

Chapter Eleven

"Aunt Cora, you seem fine now. I really think I should go help hunt food for us. Father—"

"You will not. Your father doesn't expect you to kill a buffalo to feed me." She twisted in her seat and took hold of Mary's chin. "You have much to learn." She let go and turned away. "I fear I'm not going to have enough time to teach you."

"You only need to tell me how to keep from being married. The rest I can figure out. Besides, as long as you eat, you'll be here a long time." Mary patted her aunt on the hand, and then rose.

Her aunt grabbed her. "It's not what you would expect. What if I told you I wanted to be married?"

"But you always said. . ." She plopped onto the seat.

"That's what I wanted you to believe. I made my choice and had to live with it." She dabbed her eyes. "Growing old alone isn't joyful. You'd do well to remember that."

"I still don't understand. You talk about laughing with friends and missing trains in Spain—"

"I'll tell you about that if you promise not to hunt with the men."

Guilt slid down her spine. She wanted to know more about her aunt's life, but what of her promise to her father?

Miss Periwinkle edged her way into the seat in front of them. "Did you hear? The train behind us will be here soon. I overheard some men discussing it in the observation car. They thought with the snowstorm it wouldn't have left Topeka, but it did. It's the legislature train, and it has a sleeper car. We won't have to search for comfort on these hard seats tonight."

"Why would they let us have the berths, Miss Periwinkle?" Mary tried to follow the logic of someone giving up a place to lay flat. She rubbed her neck and wished she could do the same for her lower back.

"We're women, silly. Of course we will get to use them. The legislative train is full of men. Isn't it grand being a woman?" Miss Periwinkle leaned over and checked her reflection in the window. She patted a stray hair back into place. "I must let Mr. Cross know. I'm sure he hasn't a clue since he's out scavenging for food."

Mary seethed. The woman vexed her with her all-knowing attitude and obvious attraction to Wyatt. But why? If Mary wasn't interested in him, she ought not care if Miss Periwinkle thought him a good catch.

But she did. Mary considered Wyatt's concern for her aunt. Family must be important to him. He was quick to provide for the two of them, also something good to have in a husband. He must care for adventure, since he reported the news from places like this excursion. And there was the matter of how he made her feel when he pulled her close.

But would Wyatt want Miss Periwinkle, the flirt? She had to know he wouldn't be able to afford to outfit her in expensive clothes like she now wore. Mary wouldn't need such things. Her father had plenty of money, so she wouldn't go without, even if she convinced him to follow her desire for adventure by becoming a missionary. God called her to be more than a wife. She knew it in her heart.

"You might want to let the other women in the train know first. They will be ecstatic about this as well. Run along, dear." Aunt Cora moved her legs to the side as Miss Periwinkle exited.

"I imagine they'll have provisions to share, too, Aunt Cora." Mary leaned back in her seat. The weight of her promise to her father slipped off her shoulders, leaving room for excitement to take hold. "Now tell me about the man you didn't marry."

Aunt Cora's eyes shone with the sparkle of tears.

"MR. CROSS. MR. CROSS."

Wyatt turned from the men he'd gathered to hunt small game. Miss Periwinkle stood at the top of the stairs, bundled in a fur coat. It wasn't that cold. What did she want with him? Maybe if he ignored her, she'd go back inside. "I'll go with Johnson if he promises not to shoot me. He does work for a rival paper."

"Mr. Cross!"

The woman's voice triggered a bolt of pain in his head. He waved. Maybe that would quiet her for a moment. "I'd better find out what she wants before she slides off those steps."

"I hear she's looking for a husband." Johnson guffawed.

"I'll make sure to introduce the two of you later."

Johnson snickered. "I think it's too late for me. She's set her hook for you, Cross."

"Well, I'm not getting reeled in." He'd made it clear, or so he thought, that he wasn't interested in her. Miss Periwinkle was meant for someone else. Unlike Mary, who tugged at his heart.

Heavy snow clung to his boots, impeding his progress, but the weight of his reluctance further shortened his stride.

"Mr. Cross, you don't have to go hunting," she yelled from the top step. "Another train is on its way. We've been saved."

He stopped. "Thank you, Miss Periwinkle. I need to inform the men. It was kind of you to let us know."

"You'll be coming back on the train soon, won't you, Mr. Cross?" Her lashes fluttered, lips curved—a pose no doubt meant to draw him in.

"At some point I will. You best go back inside where you'll be warm." _And far away from me._

"WHY MUST YOU KNOW?" Aunt Cora's eyes pooled with tears.

Mary wanted to cry with her aunt. She hated upsetting her. "It's only because I admire you so much. I want to be like you and travel, maybe become a missionary. Did you know one woman changed an entire village just by showing them what soap can do? Can you imagine? I want to do something with my life, like Susan Blow. Opening the kindergarten in St. Louis is such a worthy adventure." She stopped and took a breath.

"I didn't want the life I have. It's what was left when a carriage accident took the love of my life."

Mary gasped. "You were planning on getting married?"

"Yes, and it isn't as horrific a thing as you have imagined. Horace and I were going to marry that spring and live in the house my parents gave us. The one I live in now." She caressed her cheek. "We had grand plans. He was a lawyer, and we wanted to have children and take them abroad. We felt it important for children to experience the world."

"But how did you escape marriage to someone else? Every woman must marry or become the old spinster aunt."

Aunt Cora's eyebrow raised. "Providing there are other siblings. You, my dear Mo, will never be an aunt if you don't marry, since you don't have any siblings."

A cloak of loneliness settled on Mary.

"Once Horace was gone, I knew I couldn't love another, and my father didn't insist." Her aunt wiped her eyes. "I thank my father for that. He gave me a precious gift. He sent me on a tour of Europe. I traveled the world. I met so many people and made friends everywhere. Though, I think Father thought I'd return with my grieving finished and willing to marry."

"All those you met, and yet you never found another Horace?" Mary rested against the back of the bench.

"No. There were a few who came close, but they didn't make me as happy as Horace."

"Do you think it's like that for everyone? That you only get one chance at true love?" Worry crept through her. Had she passed up her chance by insisting she didn't want to marry? Is this what her father wanted her to understand, that real love only happens once? Thinking back over their conversations, Father never said she must marry, only that he desired her to.

"Maybe not everyone, but I think it is true for the Owen family. Your father felt the same about your mother. Once he lost her, he couldn't give his heart to another, not even for you, Mo. He wanted you to have a mother, but he refused to marry unless he found love again."

Mary didn't even bristle at the use of her nickname. She had much to consider, like the way Wyatt made her stomach all fluttery and her heart race when he touched her. Had God sent him? If so, what would Father think about her marrying a reporter?

Chapter Twelve

Darkness fell. Wyatt didn't reappear all afternoon, even though Miss Periwinkle told him he didn't have to hunt. The minutes continued to drag by as Miss Periwinkle chattered about all she intended to do once she reached Pueblo.

"The house Uncle purchased has thirteen bedrooms. Can you imagine, Miss Owen?"

Mary shook her head and hoped Miss Periwinkle didn't realize she'd been about to drift off. "That is quite a lot of rooms. What are you going to do with all of them?"

"Uncle hasn't said. He doesn't have any children."

Mary's stomach twisted. Something wasn't quite right. "Miss Periwinkle, why are you with your uncle instead of your parents?"

"They died. Uncle came to the door the day our house was being sold. I didn't have anywhere to go, and he was leaving the city. When he suggested I accompany him to the Colorado Territory, I was sure God sent him to rescue me. At least going with him would give me a chance to find someone else to marry." Miss Periwinkle balled her hands in her lap.

A liar. She'd told them earlier she'd been in Europe and her father let her play cards.

"You didn't know him, and you came on this trip?" Aunt Cora perked up. "I'm not sure that was wise, my dear."

"Maybe not, but I didn't have a choice. It was go with him or to the poorhouse." She sat back in the seat, and tears bubbled. "I thought my life would be different. The man I was to marry left as soon as he found out my parents died and left me without an inheritance."

"How awful, Miss Periwinkle." Mary's heart flipped from disgust to hurt. What would it be like to lose both your parents and your home?

Father wished her married, but was it really the worst thing in the world? What if she had to follow a man she didn't know to the Colorado Territory? It would be an adventure, but not one with happy excitement. Just horrible dread.

Miss Periwinkle sniffed. "Please, call me Winnie. I will be fine. I do miss my parents. Maybe when this train takes off and I get to Pueblo and see the house, I'll feel better."

Mary pulled a handkerchief from her pocket and handed it to Winnie. "What does your uncle expect you to do? Are you to be a guest? A companion? Or—"

Two men loud with laughter tumbled through the doorway; one of them landed in the lap of a woman. She shrieked.

The still-upright man dragged the other to his feet and saluted the outraged woman with a brown bottle before bringing it to his mouth and tossing back a long swig. "'Scuse me, lady. Didn't mean to land on you. Old Griff here is a bit wobbly on his feet."

Griff punched him in the arm. "You're not so stable yourself." He walked backwards and stopped next to Mary.

"What do we have here? A whole seat full of pretty women?" He reached over and grabbed Mary by the arm. "I believe red-haired beauties to be my favorite." He yanked her out of the seat.

"Stop it! Unhand me." Mary tried to peel his grip from her arm.

Miss Periwinkle screamed. "Let her go!"

Aunt Cora smacked him with her knitting needle.

Griff laughed. Snot sprayed from his nose. "Can't stop me. I'm taking her." He pulled Mary through the car and out the door. "Get the yellow-haired one for yourself. We'll have us a party, Hank."

Mary fought Griff. She couldn't get away. Why weren't any of the men helping? Where was Wyatt? *Please, God, send him to find me and Winnie!*

EVENING CREPT UP FAST on the prairie. The clear sky sparkled with stars, and the moon lit the way as Wyatt and the other men traipsed through the snow back to the train.

"Excellent idea you had, Johnson." When Johnathan suggested they explore the Kansas landscape, Wyatt agreed. The open air, though chilly, was much sweeter to him than being trapped on the train. His feet were soaked through. He didn't mind, knowing he'd soon be sitting across from Mary and warming his feet by the heat of the stove. He hoped Winnie Periwinkle had returned to her seat.

"Sorry we kept you away from your admirer. Perhaps by now she's found someone else." Johnson smacked Wyatt on the back. "Don't cry when she informs you there is another."

"She's waiting for you, Johnson. You can find a preacher in Pueblo. Maybe acquire a positon at another paper as well."

"And let you have the run at the best stories in Topeka without competition? No. I don't think so. Looks like the other train made it."

Wyatt nodded. "That should ease the tension around here. Might be some good interviews on that train, too, with all those legislators."

"I hope there is more than one. Too many reporters on board." Johnathan paused in his tracks. "Let's head over there together. I like you, Wyatt. Hate to fight you for a story."

"Excellent idea. I want to check on Miss Owen and her aunt first."

"Don't take long."

"Why don't you come with me? Give you a chance to meet Miss Periwinkle." Wyatt couldn't help the cat's-got-you grin he knew crept across his face, though his chapped lips didn't care for the too-tight stretch. He brushed his gloved finger across them, hoping they hadn't split.

"Might as well, but I imagine she's already found a man or two to talk to on the other train."

"Then you'll not be in any danger of being married by morning." Wyatt turned back to look at another group of men following them who'd stopped at the stationmaster's home to return the borrowed guns. "If we hurry, we can beat the rest of them."

MARY CONTINUED TO FIGHT Griff. The man had skin of leather. Her nails did no more than leave a red mark. Winnie had been right about there being a place to sleep on a different car. "Why are you doing this?"

"You know why, sweetheart. No need to pretend to be the innocent here." He pushed her into a sleeping berth. She fell backwards. "Paid good money for you. Could have had the other one for free, but I like that red hair. I like fighting women." He reached for her hat.

She kicked him in the chest.

He rubbed the spot where her foot landed and then laughed. "Yes, I do. And I've got me one."

He grabbed the hem of her skirt. "Let's see what color your pretty petticoat is. I bet it's red to match your shiny hair."

Mary screamed and yanked her skirt from his hand. The fabric ripped at the seam.

"Making it easier for me, aren't you, wench?" Griff licked his lips.

Mary sickened. If she'd eaten more, she would throw up on him. Instead, bile stung her throat. "Get away from me or I'll shoot." She went for the gun in her skirt pocket.

Griff pushed her down and landed on top of her, pinning her arm to her side. "Yes, indeed. I do like a woman who fights."

His wet mouth moved against the side of her neck. His beard rasped against her skin.

Mary gagged. *Dear God, please send Wyatt!*

Chapter Thirteen

The train looked homey to Wyatt with its flickering lights reflecting on the snow. *Homey? Since when had he ever had a thought like that?*

Since Mary. He should have asked her to come with him, but then she would have been the only woman, unless he'd also asked Miss Periwinkle. He shuddered. Better that he hadn't. While Mary would have enjoyed the long walk in the snow, Miss Periwinkle would have complained and made everyone miserable.

He went first up the train stairs; Johnson followed.

George didn't greet them. Odd. The hairs on Wyatt's arms tingled against his skin. High-pitched conversational cadence filled the air. Something was wrong. The car stilled when he entered. Mary's aunt slumped in her seat. Was she ill again? Where was Mary?

"Where's Miss Owen?" Perhaps George went to locate her.

"Some man drug her out of here." A gray-haired woman palmed her chest. "She fought him, but he seemed to expect that. I wouldn't have thought—"

"Mildred, be still." The older man sitting with her grasped her hand. "Someone should have stopped him."

"Where's George? Why didn't he step in?" Wyatt's tapped his foot. He had to find her.

"Haven't seen him in a while. Someone said he was getting food for our car from the other train." The older man coughed. "They pulled those girls out of this car. Went right past us, but I'm too frail. I couldn't stop them with this wretched knee."

"There was more than one? Who else did they take?" Johnson's words were hot on Wyatt's neck.

"That flirtatious Miss Periwinkle." The woman scowled.

Mary's aunt stood. "Thank goodness you're here, Mr. Cross. Did you find her?"

The car swayed under Wyatt as he rushed up the aisle to her. "No. I didn't know she was missing until now."

"What will I tell her father? I shouldn't have brought her with me. He was right." Her face was the color of chalk. "She isn't skilled enough to protect herself on an adventure like this."

"Did you know the men that took them?" Wyatt settled her back onto the seat.

"No. You have to find them. They were evil. Smelled of whiskey. Please hurry."

Where would they have taken Mary? His stomach sunk as he remembered Winnie telling him about the sleeping car. This time of day it would be empty. The perfect place to hide malevolent activity. "Come on, Johnathan. We have evil to stomp."

"Someone make sure she gets something to eat." Wyatt yelled as he pounded back through the car to the door. "You." He pointed at the older man. "You can do that much."

MARY STRUGGLED UNDERNEATH Griff. He smelled like old fish and hair tonic. There had to be a way to get away from him. She couldn't get to her gun, and it didn't matter as it wasn't loaded. Wiggling to one side, she freed her hand. She grabbed a hunk of Griff's hair and yanked.

"Ow! What'd you do that for?" He put his face close to hers and gave a reptilian wink. "I think you're asking for more excitement than you're ready for, missy."

A shadow cast by the gas lights wavered against the wall. Did Mary dare hope?

Griff's weight left her body. She scrambled off the bed to the dull beat of punches connecting with solid mass.

Wyatt landed a glancing right cross off of Griff's chin. He forced him down the narrow aisle away from her. "Get out now, Mary."

Her legs wobbled. She hung on to the curtain of the booth while the car spun. There were two Wyatts and two Griffs.

"You've made a mistake messing with this woman." Wyatt guarded his chin with a raised fist.

"But I paid for her." Griff snapped out a head shot, but Wyatt ducked left and blocked his attack.

"Then you were scammed. She isn't for sale." Wyatt threw his weight behind one final gut punch. "No woman should be bought."

Wyatt's fist connected, and Griff rocked back against the wall, chest doubled over his knees.

Wyatt turned and grabbed Mary, holding her close to his chest. "Did he hurt you?"

The car stopped spinning. She breathed in Wyatt's scent. He'd come for her, protected her. She burst into tears.

WYATT HELD MARY CLOSE. What if he hadn't arrived in time?

"Winnie. Wyatt, that other man took her." She broke free of his embrace, steady in her gaze. "We have to find her."

"My friend Johnson is looking for her. I hope he found her as easily as I found you. We split up to check the cars."

"You came in time. He was so. . ." She sniffled.

"Shh. You don't have to talk about it. Unless you want to." If she filled in any details, he might have to shoot the man groaning on the floor.

"No. I want to forget what happened. Thank you for rescuing me."

Wyatt stroked Mary's back. He hated tears, but she had every right to bawl her eyes out. She clung to him, and a protective side he hadn't known he possessed stirred. He vowed to keep her safe the rest of the trip.

Just the trip? He didn't want to admit it, but he loved this outlaw.

Chapter Fourteen

Mary and Wyatt discovered Winnie and Johnson in the next car. Winnie's face held a tinge of green, and her hair resembled a haystack that had been repeatedly stabbed by a pitchfork. Then again, Mary considered she might not look her best either, what with her ripped skirt. She hugged Winnie. "I'm so glad you're okay."

"Had to bang up your man, too, I see, Johnson." Wyatt glared at the man on the floor. "I left the other vermin in the car. We should see someone about getting them locked up."

"Mary, your skirt." Winnie's lips trembled. "And me, a mess. How are we going to go back in our car? Everyone will stare."

"We will march in there and sit by Aunt Cora and let her fuss over us. No one jumped up to save us from these men. Let them see what damage they wrought."

Winnie's eyes widened. "Johnson found me in time. Didn't Wyatt?"

"In time for what?" Had Winnie's attacker hit her on the head?

"To protect your virtue."

Red-pepper heat blossomed across Mary's face. "Shh." She turned to see if Wyatt heard.

"Johnson, help me drag this one next door. I'll keep them in there until you find out where we need to put them. I'm thinking the caboose would be the spot where someone could watch them until we reach Pueblo."

"Why don't we drag them there now, before they get their wits about them and start swinging?"

"Good idea. Ladies, can you make your way back to your car?"

"Yes, we can." Winnie braided her hair. "As soon as we feel presentable."

Wyatt touched Mary on the shoulder. "How about you? I should escort you back to your aunt."

"No, I'd rather see those men contained somewhere as soon as possible." Her heart skipped a beat. He cared about her.

Once the men left, Mary turned to Winnie and tucked a piece of her hair back into her bun. "That's better. About what you asked. Wyatt did reach me in time."

Winnie sighed. "We are fortunate to have been saved."

"Yes, but if you thought what you did, will the others think that, too, because of my skirt?"

Winnie stepped back. "Let me see. Turn for me."

Mary did a slow revolution. White fabric peeked out of the tear. "What am I going to do?"

"I can help." Winnie pulled up the hem of her dress. "See, I pinned my petticoat because it was too long. We can use the pins on your skirt."

"But then yours will drag below your hem."

"I don't care. The older women will think I'm sloppy, nothing more. But the tear in your garment will cause titters for sure and damage your reputation."

"Thank you, Winnie." Mary's heart softened. She was sorry for judging Winnie as selfish and uncaring for eating her aunt's cake.

"It's okay. You would do the same for me."

"Why didn't your uncle help us?" Mary tried to remember. Was he in the car when they were taken?

"He's not my uncle." Winnie hiccupped a sob. "He said he was a friend of my father's. He's awful, Mary. What he wants me to do. . . I can't, I just can't. I won't."

"You won't have to. Aunt Cora and I will find a way to save you."

"Can you find me a husband before we get to Pueblo?"

Wyatt. Would he marry Winnie? He did make a dandy rescuer. But could Mary stand by and watch him wed another? It would be an act of kindness a missionary would do. Maybe she wasn't strong enough to be one after all.

MARY EXPLAINED TO HER aunt what happened in such a way so no one overheard the conversation. Winnie sat across from them, hugging the window.

"There is no way, Miss Periwinkle, that you are going to sit with that man or go anywhere with him once we reach Pueblo." Cora's voice rose.

"Shh, Aunt!"

Cora lowered her voice. "You will travel with us and then return to St. Louis."

"He has my luggage tag. He said I wouldn't get it back if I tried to run off. I don't have money to replace my clothing."

"Never you mind. If he refuses to give it to me and Mr. Cross, then I'll provide you with a new wardrobe."

Wyatt? Had she decided he would be a good match for Winnie? Mary squirmed in her seat. "Father will help her, I'm sure."

Aunt Cora gave her a knowing look. "I am positive of that, but he won't be in Pueblo when we arrive. Mr. Cross has proved himself useful in certain situations. It won't hurt to ask him for assistance in this manner."

Mary sat back. She couldn't argue with her aunt because she was right. Wyatt was all that her aunt said and more.

"If you'll excuse me, I'm going to the women's lounge." Winnie scooted to the edge of the seat.

"Would you like me to come with you?" Mary wasn't sure her new friend should go anywhere alone.

"I'll be fine."

Winnie left the car, and Mary turned to her aunt. "Do you want her to marry Mr. Cross?"

"Would that bother you?"

"I don't know. No. Yes. Aunt Cora, I'm conflicted. I want to be missionary, but I find myself desiring Wyatt's company."

"Again, tell me, why do you insist on being a missionary?"

"To help."

"You can choose to help from anywhere. Missionaries need support from those of us who aren't living in Africa and India. Even today, offering to help Winnie is a mission act. What kind of things could you do if you married Wyatt and lived in Topeka?"

"He hasn't proposed, Aunt Cora. And then there is Father. He won't approve." She considered what her aunt said. She was right. Missionaries had come to her school to speak and raise money. Maybe she and Wyatt could visit one of the countries so they could speak with authorities and then raise money or even collect soap and send it back. That is, if he asked her to marry him.

WYATT TESTED THE ROPE that tied Griff's wrist to the bunk in the caboose. Both men sobered and expressed regret, but that wasn't enough for Wyatt to let them go.

"Why did you choose them in the first place?" He stepped back. They wouldn't be going anywhere, especially since he and Johnson decided to take shifts watching them.

"The blonde's uncle said we could have them. He said the blonde would be available in Pueblo, that he wanted to start his business early."

Wyatt clenched his hand into a tight fist, then forced it to relax. He couldn't bring himself to hit a tied-up man no matter how much he wanted to.

"Those are respectable women. You were misinformed."

"Tell them we're sorry. Griff and I were playing cards and drinking with the girl's uncle. When he lost, he offered them to us instead of money."

"That will be the last time he does that." Wyatt settled in with his notebook on a hard bench. "Tell me what you know about him."

Chapter Fifteen

Wyatt's neck hurt. He'd spent too much time guarding the prisoners. The swaying of the train beneath him coaxed and cajoled him to close his eyes. The engineer had received the all clear that morning, and the excursion to Pueblo resumed. There were many cheers of joy rumbling through the coaches.

He and Johnson decided to spend the last night of the trip watching the two men rather than split the time. The caboose had two unoccupied beds that were more comfortable than the seats in the cars, making it a cozy nook for him and Johnson to discuss the state of the world.

"Johnson, with the trains going to more places, there are going to be more towns springing up and newspapers needing reporters. Have you ever thought about moving west?"

"You suggesting something? Trying to oust the competition?"

"No, just thinking aloud. I'd like to try another city or town, but I plan to stay in Topeka." Was Mary still sleeping? He'd popped into her car to check on her and found her resting against the window. She had to be cold. He wanted to pick her up and move her closer to the stove. But he didn't have the right.

"Not me—I want to see the world. All the little towns with their crazy lawlessness will make for great stories. Might even send them to New York for the big papers." Johnson yawned. His voice lowered and slowed as the night wore on.

Wyatt slid off the bottom berth and gazed out the window. The sky sparkled with millions of stars. He wanted to show it to Mary.

He nudged Johnson's foot. "Wake up. I'm taking a little walk."

Johnson snorted. "Checking on your woman again?"

"Yes, I suppose I am."

"MARY, ARE YOU AWAKE?"

She jumped. Stopped a scream from escaping her lips when she realized it was Wyatt who touched her. "Is something wrong?" She sat up and rubbed her eyes. The train still moved, Aunt Cora gave a ladylike snore, and Winnie—well, she had a line of drool on her chin. Mary quickly wiped her own just in case.

"Will you come with me to the observation car?" Wyatt whispered.

She blinked, then stood, responding to his request before she processed the thought in her mind.

"I understand if you are afraid, but there are others there. We won't be alone." He held out his hand to help steady her as she stepped over Aunt Cora.

In silence, they made their way to the car. Wyatt spoke the truth. There were several people in the car, all staring out the windows.

Wyatt pulled her to an empty space. "Isn't it beautiful?"

Outside, the moon and stars shimmered on what appeared to be a large lake. The reflections of the dancing stars took her breath. "It's the most amazing sight. Thank you, Wyatt, for waking me. We should have woken Aunt Cora and Winnie, too."

"No. I mean, there's something I wanted to ask you without them being present." He pulled her close to him and whispered in her ear. "I know we haven't known each other long, but I feel in my heart that you are the woman God chose for me."

"Wyatt—"

"Shh." He traced her cheekbone. "I've fallen in love with you and want to marry you, spend the rest of my life with you. I want to take you to Yellowstone for our honeymoon. They've opened a hotel there. I think you'd like to see water fountains that shoot from the earth. So, would you be my wife?"

Her heart beat so hard she felt it would break through her chest. He loved her. Despite what almost happened with Griff and that she could shoot better than he could. He wanted to take her on adventures, not leave her at home. She considered what Aunt Cora had said about being a missionary wherever she lived.

"Mary?"

"I want to marry you, Wyatt. I have dreams of helping those in need. Would you be willing to let me do that?"

"What do you mean?"

"I want to be a missionary, but I don't have to travel. Though I'd like to, even though this trip was a bit more exciting than I expected. I want to raise money to help missionary families."

"I'll join you. We'll go to India, if you like."

He would, too. Warmth spread though her. "Yes, Wyatt, I'll marry you, if my father approves." She lowered her chin and canted her body until her forehead rested against his chest.

He didn't move.

She stayed there, feeling the rise and fall of his breath. "He won't, though, because you're a reporter."

She felt a gentle kiss on the top of her head. Had anyone seen? It didn't matter, because the star show was nothing like the fireworks bursting inside her.

"What if Father says you can't marry me?"

"Don't worry. He will approve, as will mine."

"How do you know?" Mary twisted her fingers together.

"Because my full name is William Wyatt Crossen. My father owns a large shipping company, and I'm his heir."

She stepped back. "I don't understand. You lied to me? And what will our last name be? What am I to call you?"

He scratched his head. "My father insisted I shorten our surname when I became a reporter to distance himself. I've always liked Wyatt better."

"You'll have to figure this out before you speak to my father."

A satisfied smile lit Wyatt's face. "So, you will marry me." He drew her close and kissed her.

Mary's knees knocked, weak as a newborn kitten's. She might have even purred.

AT THE PUEBLO STATION, weary-looking musicians played as the passengers disembarked from the train. There were signs and street vendors everywhere even though the train arrived late.

"Aunt Cora, this is amazing. What it must be like to be greeted like this at the end of every great adventure." Mary twisted from side to side to take in as much of the festivities as possible.

"If you have a family to return to, it is like this without the vendors and massive crowds. But it's even more special to be greeted by someone who loves you. Winnie, you're staying with us at the hotel. Mr. Cross is making sure your luggage is sent to our rooms."

"I don't know how to thank you and Mary for taking me in." Winnie stood taller and her smile appeared softer, not forced as it had been on the first part of their trip.

Mary hooked arms with Winnie. "Think of yourself as my sister."

"No, I think she'll be the cousin you didn't have." Aunt Cora beamed. "I didn't have a chance to have a child. I'm taking Winnie for my own. My brother has his child, and now I have mine."

Winnie turned to Mary. "Is that okay with you?"

"Yes, of course! Sister, cousin—at this point in our lives, either would be perfect. But you must promise to look after my father, too, after I marry Wyatt. If I marry him."

"But you must! He's such a gentleman, and he loves you. Everyone can see that."

"First, he has to decide who he is, and Father has to give his blessing." And that she wasn't so sure about. He didn't care for people who lied or for newspaper men.

Chapter Sixteen

Mary paced the floor of her upstairs bedroom back home in St. Louis. She missed the excitement of traveling with Aunt Cora. Now Winnie went with her. It didn't feel right that she was left behind. Even Wyatt had disappeared after he spoke to her father about marriage. Some things he had to do, he'd said. What would she do if he never returned?

She pulled the curtain aside and saw a carriage pull up. Wyatt stepped out. Her heart thudded. He came. She ran for the stairs, then stopped at the top. She couldn't very well greet him like her father's pet dog. She backed against the wall and waited an eternity for her father to call for her.

"Mo, please come down."

She wasted no time bouncing down the stairs, light as air. "Yes, Father?"

He tweaked her ear. "I know you were up there waiting. Wyatt is here to speak with you." He kissed her cheek. "You have my blessing, if he suits you."

Mary entered the parlor where Wyatt waited. "You came back."

"I said I would. I need to tell you something."

"Continue."

"I've spoken to my father about continuing to write. With my mother's influence, he decided I can write under my own name, if I write for missionary magazines."

Mary's heart quickened. God was going to answer her prayer.

He knelt and grasped her hands. "I love you. Would you be my wife and accompany me on my travels to gather stories for the magazines until such a time as we have a family? Then we'll find a small town to settle."

"Yes, and I will travel wherever you go."

MARY OWEN AND WILLIAM Crossen's wedding was the event of the season and the talk of the town. Her father spared no expense, but Mary let him only after he promised to do the same for Winnie when she married.

Mary wore a white satin gown from New York instead of Paris, because she refused to wait for a dress to be made and shipped. Organ notes signaled it was time to stroll down the aisle with her father.

"Mo, I pray for a love as strong and wonderful as what your mother and I had."

"Thank you, Father." Mary wiped a tear away. "I love William, but I will miss you."

"I know." He took her arm and led her to William.

Soon it was her turn to pledge her vow. "I, Mary, take thee, Wyatt-William—"

"My little outlaw, call me Wyatt or William. I will love you forever and always."

"And I you."

THE TRAIN RUMBLED AGAINST the tracks. Steam billowed white against the blue sky. Aunt Cora and Winnie accompanied Mary and Wyatt to see them off.

"I'll find George and get our luggage settled while you say your good-byes." Wyatt tipped his hat and left.

"Mary, take care and think before you do something adventurous." Aunt Cora hugged her tightly.

"I promise. Winnie, take care of Aunt Cora and Father." She hugged Winnie. "He mentioned having a dinner for you to meet a possible husband. Don't be afraid. He was right. Marriage is wonderful. Aunt Cora, he said the same about finding you a match."

"Hmpf." Cora shook her head. "Winnie, let's host a dinner for my brother. I think he needs a wife."

Wyatt returned. "George has taken care of our belongings. Mrs. Crossen, are you ready to take our first adventure as a married couple?"

"I am. Bye, Aunt Cora and Winnie." The warmth of his hand on hers touched her heart. God had provided.

"Yellowstone, here we come. Bears, waterfalls, and geysers are the perfect way to start our life together." He squeezed her hand. "I love you, Outlaw."

"And I love you."

THANK YOU FOR JOINING the adventure with Mary Owens!

Here's a sneak peak at the next small town bride.

A Christmas Wish

She vowed to marry for love. He promised his daughters a mother for Christmas. Time is running out for both of them.

Chapter 1
Southern Illinois, 1886

Roy Gibbons stirred the pot of oatmeal on the woodstove while doing his best to ignore the state of his kitchen.

"Papa, it shouldn't look like that." Eight-year-old Elisbet glared at him. "I can't wait until our Christmas mama gets here."

If Janie were here, everything would be in the cupboards where it belonged, not shoved into nooks and crannies. He never thought he'd be making breakfast for his daughters, much less trying to keep their frocks clean and pressed. He missed his wife more and more every day. Roy didn't know how she'd made his home run so smoothly. Not once had he needed to worry about how to get tomato stains off his shirt or when to cut his hair. She'd say in her musical voice, "It's time, sit down and let me trim that head, Roy."

When Elisbet asked him for a mother for Christmas, he'd said yes, thinking it couldn't be that hard to find one.

"Papa, do you think Becky will have sugar cookies at her party?" Frances, his youngest and his shadow, tugged his pant leg.

"Franny, she's going to have cake. That's what you have at a birthday party, right, Papa?" Elisbet never had trouble correcting her younger sister.

"But I like sugar cookies." Frances tugged again. "Can we make cookies when we come home? Mama makes the best kind."

"Mama *made* not makes. She's in heaven. Remember?" Elisbet patted her sister's shoulder. "When our Christmas mama comes, she'll make cookies with us."

"Stop telling her that, Elisbet. It's not that easy to get a mother. You can't wish for a mother and I can't order one from the catalog." He slid the pot from the burner, his little shadow still clinging to his leg as he moved. "Sit down, girls, and I'll fill your bowls." Roy was still stinging from Widow Percy's rejection. She'd have been a perfect fill-in for his deceased wife. Seemed logical—she didn't have a father for her boys, and his girls didn't have a mother. When he suggested they marry for the common good of their families, she'd done all but slap his face.

Trouble was, he hadn't lived here long enough to know people. Maybe he'd made a mistake moving here after Janie died. If he'd stayed in Collinsville, he'd have a mother for the girls by now. The whole reason he'd left was because too many young hopefuls were knocking on the door with some treat and mooning over him and the girls. At the time he didn't want another wife. No one could fill Janie's shoes, and these women would be expecting to have children of their own. He couldn't face that, not after losing Janie and the baby. No, he didn't need a companion. Just someone to take care of his house and his family.

He scooped up the oatmeal and plopped a lump in each girl's bowl.

He sat at the head of the table, a daughter on either side of him, and pushed back the hurt that came from seeing Janie's chair at the other end. The house was different, but the spot across the table was as empty as if he hadn't left Collinsville. "Grace, then food." He watched until little hands were folded and heads bowed, then said the prayer followed by an "Amen."

Frances stuck her fingers on the inside of her bowl to pull it closer. "Hot!" The bowl went spinning from the table to her lap and then crashed to the floor. She wailed.

"Are you all right? Are your fingers burned?" Roy sprung from his chair and pulled his daughter from hers. He grabbed her hands and flipped them palm up. They weren't red. Relieved to avoid a crisis, he planted a kiss on her fingertips the way he'd seen Janie do so many times.

"My dress," Frances whimpered. "It's dirty. I don't have another one for the party."

"Shh, Frances, stop crying. Your fingers look fine, and no one will notice your dress." Kneeling, he reached under the table for the offending bowl and spoon that had spoiled Frances's morning.

"If we had a mama, this wouldn't have happened, Papa." Elisbet already held a wet rag in her hand. She dabbed at her sister's dress. "It's only a little bit of oatmeal. Look, Franny. See? I got it off."

It bothered him that Elisbet tried to be like Janie, and he had no idea how to prevent it.

"But it's my favorite and it's. . ." Frances hiccupped. "Wet!"

Roy wondered how he would ever raise these girls without help.

ALMA PICKENS TUGGED her cape closer to guard against the sharp fangs of the November wind and leaned across the buggy seat. Her father had returned to the very subject she'd asked him not to speak about at breakfast. "Papa, you're a dreamer. Maybe I'm not the only one God will send a spouse for. I do believe I'll pray as hard as you do for me, that you'll marry again. A doctor should have a wife."

And she would take it to God in her prayers. She'd grown weary of her father's constant efforts to see her married. It wasn't that she was against the idea, but she'd made a promise to her mother to take care of him. And it would be a rare man who would marry her and take in her father as well.

Besides, she had her painting and taking care of her father's home. That gave her plenty to do. Why, just this morning she'd risen earlier than normal and put in a full day's work so she could come to town with him despite the cold to make a deposit at the bank and to visit her friend Jewel.

"Little Bit, it's not right for you to devote your life to me."

"Papa, I told you not to worry about me. I have you, and I don't need anyone else. Besides, there isn't anyone left in Trenton that I'd care to marry."

"Alma my girl, you'll make a good wife and mother. I can't sit back and watch you miss out. God will bring someone." He stopped the horse in front of Bossman's Bank and stepped out of the wagon. He tied the horse to the hitching post and helped

Alma dismount. "I'm too old to get married again. It's you I worry about. I'll pick you up at Jewel's when I'm through at the Detterman's. And don't start making lists of promising wives for me. Go on, get in the bank and put your pennies away."

"I'm going." Who would be a good match for him? And who could she find that wouldn't mind her presence in the house as well?

Maybe she should hold off ordering from the Montgomery Ward catalog. She had her heart set on the Oil Painting Outfit Complete. It was outrageously expensive, but it came with twenty-five colors of paint. If she weren't able to sell her paintings right away, and her father married a woman who valued their privacy, she would need that money to rent a room somewhere. And without the paints and lessons that came with the painting outfit, how would she have anything to sell? Well, she wouldn't worry about that today, seeing as how there weren't any women who interested Papa. The irony that this town held no one for either of them struck her. Maybe Papa would consider moving to St. Louis, where her paintings would be discovered, and she'd be famous and wealthy. He could be a doctor there, and the number of people in that city would increase his chance of finding another wife.

She needed to talk this new idea of St. Louis over with Jewel. Together they'd find a solution.

INSIDE THE BANK, ALMA waited her turn. Two little blond girls in front of her clung to their father. She knew who they were—the Gibbons family minus the mother who had died last spring giving birth. Mrs. Remik at the store said everyone was speculating on when Mr. Gibbons would take another wife to help with Elisbet and Frances.

The oldest, Elisbet, played peekaboo with her sister. Their giggles captured one hiding in Alma. She clenched her lips to contain it, but it escaped.

Mr. Gibbons turned and smiled. Alma had an unusual urge to slide her finger into the indentation on his cheek. Dimples. Then she noticed what looked like oatmeal in his hair. She shuddered. The man needed help.

"I apologize if my girls disturbed you, miss."

"They didn't. Their giggles captivated me along with those dark blue eyes." If she were painting them, she'd use cobalt blue to capture their intensity.

"We're going to a birthday party," Elisbet said.

Alma leaned down. "I love birthday parties, lots of games and cake to eat."

"I have oatmeal on my dress." Frances looked so sorrowful that Alma wanted to take her down to the store and buy her a new frock.

"Franny, it's okay. Remember I got it off and your dress dried on the way here. Papa, we have to get Becky a gift, don't forget. I want to get her red hair ribbons."

Had that man brought his daughter out in this cold weather with a wet dress? Was he touched in the head? No doubt her own father would end up at their place tending to the little girl for pneumonia.

"I don't. I think we should get her a knife." Frances held up her hands and pretended to open one. "It would be grand to have one. Papa, can I have one for my birthday?"

"We'll see. We best get moving if there's shopping and lunch to do yet." He turned to Alma. "Nice to meet you."

"Papa, can she be the mama you're getting us for Christmas? She doesn't have a wedding ring. I looked like you showed me." Elisbet smiled a got-you-now smile at her father.

Mr. Gibbons's green eyes flashed to Alma's, and his face flushed. "Let's go, girls." He ushered them out without another word to Alma.

Alma watched them leave, noticing the hem on Elisbet's coat was torn. She understood the child's desire for a mother but sincerely hoped her father didn't run into Mr. Gibbons before Christmas.

Start reading A Christmas Wish now!

Visit Dana at DianaBrandmeyer.com

Historical

Small Town Brides

Love Finds an Outlaw

The Christmas Wish

The Matchmaker Bride

The Honey Bride

From a Distance

Frontier Legacy Brides

A Bride's Dilemma in Friendship, Tennessee

A Bride's Journey to the Colorado Territory

A Bride's Choice in Central City

Contemporary

Silverton Series

All in Good Time

A Time to Dance

A Time to Bake

A Time to Heal

A Time to Love contains A Time to Dance, A Time to Bake and A Time to Heal

Stand Alone Books

Mind of Her Own

Hearts on the Road

About the Author

Diana Lesire Brandmeyer writes historical and contemporary romances. She is the best-selling author of *Mind of Her Own, Frontier Legacy Brides series,* and *The Silverton Lake Romance series.* Once widowed and now remarried, she writes with humor and experience on the difficulty of joining two families, be it fictional or real life.

Please visit her webpage, www.dianabrandmeyer.com

.

Don't miss out!

Visit the website below and you can sign up to receive emails whenever Diana Lesire Brandmeyer publishes a new book. There's no charge and no obligation.

https://books2read.com/r/B-A-RBRD-XXPLB

www.ingramcontent.com/pod-product-compliance
Lightning Source LLC
Chambersburg PA
CBHW031352060726
47590CB00007B/2749